6/17

BAND GEEKS

Band Camp Rules

Calico

An Imprint of Magic Wagon
abdopublishing.com

by Amy Cobb
Illustrated by Anna Cattish

For every Band Geek who fills our world with beautiful music. And with sincerest gratitude to Mr. Vaught, who has instilled a love of music in the hearts of many. —AC

abdopublishing.com

Published by Magic Wagon, a division of ABDO,
PO Box 398166, Minneapolis, Minnesota 55439.
Copyright © 2017 by Abdo Consulting Group, Inc.
International copyrights reserved in all countries. No part of this
book may be reproduced in any form without written permission from
the publisher. Calico™ is a trademark and logo of Magic Wagon.

Printed in the United States of America, North Mankato, Minnesota.
102016
012017

Written by Amy Cobb
Illustrated by Anna Cattish
Edited by Megan M. Gunderson
Designed by Christina Doffing
Art Directed by Candice Keimig

Publisher's Cataloging-in-Publication Data

Names: Cobb, Amy, author. | Cattish, Anna, illustrator.
Title: Band camp rules / by Amy Cobb ; illustrated by Anna Cattish.
Description: Minneapolis, MN : Magic Wagon, 2017. | Series: Band geeks
Summary: Morgan Bryant wants to be a leader, but she struggles to lead
    the clarinet section at summer arts camp.
Identifiers: LCCN 2016947361 | ISBN 9781624021725 (lib. bdg.) |
    ISBN 9781624022326 (ebook) | ISBN 9781624022623 (Read-to-me
    ebook)
Subjects: LCSH: Music camps--Juvenile fiction. | Bands (Music)--
    Juvenile fiction. | Junior high schools--Juvenile fiction. | Middle
    schools--Juvenile fiction.
Classification: DDC [Fic]--dc23
LC record available at http://lccn.loc.gov/2016947361

TABLE OF CONTENTS

Chapter 1

BUT NO S'MORES?

Room 217. I ran my fingers across the plastic letters on the nameplate just outside the door. BAND ROOM. A bunch of students had gathered in the hallway waiting for Mr. Byrd, our band director, to arrive.

"Can you believe it?" I asked. "Our first year of junior high school at Benton Bluff hasn't officially started yet, and here we are!"

"I'm super excited, Morgan!" Carmen Trochez squealed.

Our friend Colby Ellis smiled and chimed in with, "Me too!"

"Puh-lease," Tally Nguyen mumbled. "I'd rather be sleeping. That's what summer break was invented for."

I glanced at my watch. "But it's two o'clock in the afternoon."

"I know," Tally said.

"Nah, summer break was invented for fishing," Zac Wiles chimed in. "I wish I were at the lake. The fish are probably biting like crazy today."

I didn't know about the fish, but I was pretty sure Tally and Zac were both a little wacko. I met them a few weeks ago at Orientation Night for seventh graders. Only, they weren't there to be oriented. They were there with the other eighth graders to welcome us to the band.

After that night, Mr. Byrd had called our parents to talk about us helping out with a special summer project. I wasn't sure what it involved, but I couldn't wait to find out.

"Aren't you guys excited? A little?" I asked.

"No way!" Zac said. "Summer vacation means a break from school, including band. Doesn't Mr. Byrd get it?"

"Sure, I get it that it's summer vacation, Zac," Mr. Byrd said, coming up behind us.

Zac's face turned as red as the sunset on Mr. Byrd's palm-tree-covered shirt. So far, every time I'd seen Mr. Byrd, he wore khaki shorts and a tropical shirt, paired with flip-flops and topped with a straw hat. He looked more like a beachgoer than a Band Geek.

"But summer break doesn't mean musicians take a break from making music," Mr. Byrd continued. "In fact, summer is the perfect season for nature to spark our musical creativity. Think of croaking bullfrogs, chirping crickets, or a crackling bonfire for a weenie roast. That's all music, Zac!"

"Hey, my fellow bandmates, guess what else makes music," Sherman Frye said, not waiting for anyone to answer. "Here's a hint. It's brown, white, and gooey, and it crunches when you bite into it."

"Anything my mom cooks is brown and crunchy when you bite into it," Zac joked.

Everyone laughed, even Mr. Byrd. Then he said, "We give up, Sherman. What's the answer to your riddle?"

"S'mores!" Sherman said. "Get it? Chocolate and gooey white marshmallows sandwiched between crunchy graham crackers."

"Stop! You're making me hungry," Davis Beadle and Zac said at the same time.

And Hope James said, "What do s'mores have to do with anything, Sherman? That makes, like, zero sense."

"It makes total sense," Sherman said, his curly brown hair bobbing up and down as he talked. "Mr. Byrd was talking about frogs and crickets and weenie roasts." He folded his arms across his chest. "Hello! Who has a bonfire without s'mores?"

Hope shook her head, laughing.

"Wait a minute!" Sherman went on. "I think I'm onto something here. Are you taking us on a camping trip, Mr. Byrd?"

"Not exactly," Mr. Byrd said. "But sort of, and I need everyone's help."

"Help with what?" Baylor asked.

Baylor played clarinet, same instrument as me. She was super nice at Orientation Night. And I already knew she asked a ton of questions. Probably because she was also a reporter for the school newspaper, the *Benton Bluff Bloodhound*.

Mr. Byrd unlocked the band room and smiled as he motioned us inside. "That's what we're here to discuss."

Even though I'd been in room 217 a few times now, the band room still gave me goose bumps. The chairs were arranged on levels, sort of like a movie theater. Except instead of a big screen, Mr. Byrd's podium was the focus of the room. That's where he'd stand to direct us when band actually started in a few more weeks. I could hardly wait!

But the most exciting part was the trophies spotlighted in a glass case on one wall. Being a part of such a talented band was an honor. And I hoped that while I was a student in the band, even more trophies would be added to that case.

"How can we 'sort of' go on a camping trip, Mr. Byrd?" I asked once we'd all settled in our seats.

Baylor nodded. "I was wondering that, too."

"Well," Mr. Byrd began, "like I said, summertime often sparks our musical creativity. And what better way to spark an interest in music than by having a summer camp for younger students?"

"I knew it!" Sherman practically jumped out of his chair. "We *are* going camping."

"Yes! We're finally doing something fun around here." Zac fist-bumped Davis. "My tent's got room for four people. And I have extra fishing rods."

"I'm in!" Davis said.

Sherman smiled. "Me too!"

Mr. Byrd held up his hands. "Hang on, boys. It is a camp, but no tents are required. I've spoken with your parents, and they've given permission for you all to attend a week-long day camp starting next Monday. Except, you guys won't be campers."

"Huh?" Davis said.

"That's right, Davis. You'll be counselors." Mr. Byrd pulled out a flyer. At the top it said *Benton Bluff Summer Arts Camp.*

"What does art have to do with music?" Zac asked.

Mr. Byrd's eyebrows shot up. "Everything, Zac! Music is art. Instead of painting a visual picture with a brush, the musician creates an image with a melody."

"*Oui, monsieur!* Just call me Lemuel Soriano, the great musical *artiste,*" Lem said in his best French accent.

I remembered Lem from Orientation Night, too. His family was from the Philippines, and he'd discovered some royal French ancestor. That was pretty cool, I thought. And so was the way Lem spoke in French sometimes.

"That's right, Lem." Mr. Byrd nodded. "You're all musical *artistes*, and this camp provides an opportunity for you to share your talents with younger musicians. I've already paired you in teams, according to your musical section." He pulled out another sheet of paper and read:

Drums—Davis Beadle and Carmen Trochez

Flute—Sherman Frye and Hope James

Clarinet—Morgan Bryant and Baylor Meece

Saxophone—Colby Ellis and Zac Wiles

Trumpet—Miles Darr and Lem Soriano

Trombone—Ellen Carrico and Kori Neal

French horn—Tally Nguyen and Brady Wyatt

After making the assignments, Mr. Byrd handed out some papers.

"What's all of this stuff?" Kori asked.

"This stuff," Mr. Byrd said, "is information for camp. There's sheet music that we'll practice with the campers. And there are also some activities that we'll implement to make learning fun."

I wasn't so sure about the fun part. I mean, if the campers were going to learn anything next week, they'd have to take music very seriously.

And then I wondered something. "Can we get together this weekend to work on this on our own?"

"That's a great idea!" Mr. Byrd said.

Zac fake coughed and said under his breath, "Teacher's pet."

"C'mon, Zac," I said. "We want this project to be perfect."

Zac looked like he couldn't believe it. "This whole camp thing sounds like tons of work to me."

I ignored Zac and suggested, "Maybe we can all meet here on the playground tomorrow to go over some stuff."

"That works for me," Baylor said.

"Me too," Miles chimed in.

Everyone else agreed, too. Tomorrow we'd make plans. And camp next week would be perfect. No matter what Zac said.

Chapter 2
FUN & GAMES

The next afternoon, my dad dropped me off at the school playground for our meeting.

"It looks like someone came prepared," Baylor said, pointing my way. Hope was in the swing beside her. They both lazily swung back and forth. Some of the other kids whirled on the merry-go-round. And a few more hung out on the monkey bars.

"Yeah, Morgan brought a clipboard and everything," Sherman said, heading toward us.

I smiled. "And you brought a yo-yo. Cool!"

"Check out my latest trick," Sherman said. "It's called around the corner." He flicked his yo-yo forward, and then brought it up from behind his arm and caught it again.

I clapped. "Nice!"

"Thank you!" Sherman took a bow. "I'm training to be in a contest for the world's yo-yo champion someday."

"Is that really a thing?" I asked.

Sherman frowned, like I had the nerve to even ask that question. "Of course that's really a thing," he said. "There's different divisions and everything."

"Then I hope you win," I said.

Sherman did another trick with his yo-yo. He said it was called the elevator. The yo-yo slid straight up the string, sort of like an elevator moving up in a tall building. "So," he said, putting away his yo-yo, "what about you, Morgan?"

"What about me what?" I asked.

"What do you do for fun? Besides band, I mean," he said.

"Well, I—" But then I stopped. That was a tough question. Really, I didn't have any other hobbies besides music. Playing my clarinet meant everything to me. "I guess that's it," I finally said.

"C'mon," Colby jumped in. "There's gotta be something else you like to do."

I shook my head. "Not really. But," I went on, "I do hope to be a famous bandleader someday. There aren't very many women conductors in the whole world, you know."

Sherman looked surprised. "No, I didn't know that."

"It's true." I smiled. "And you're looking at the next great conductor."

"Impressive," Colby said.

"Thanks," I said. Then I scanned the playground to see who wasn't there yet. "Are we just waiting on Zac?"

"He's always late," Baylor said.

"Always," Hope repeated.

I frowned. "I guess we can start without him. Let's head over to the picnic tables."

Sherman gave a whistle. "Over here, guys!"

He motioned everyone over and we filled a few of the tables. We'd just begun talking about the different camp activities planned for next week when Zac finally showed up.

"Let's get this over with," he said. "This whole day camp idea is dumb."

I sat down at a table and asked, "What do you have against camp, Zac?"

He looked like he was thinking about it before he finally said, "Everything!"

"Don't pay any attention to Zac," Baylor said, shaking her head. "The last band camp didn't go so great for him."

"Yeah, this one kid named Aubrey tried to make me look like I was the loser who was going around camp stealing the other kids' instruments," Zac explained.

"What?" I couldn't believe it. "Why would anyone do that?"

Zac grinned. "Probably because she was jealous of my skills."

"Seriously?" I wasn't sure if Zac was joking, so I looked at Baylor to get the truth. "Is he for real?"

"Totally." She nodded.

"That's too bad," I said. And I meant it. "But the best part is, this time, you're not a camper. Instead, you're a counselor, like Mr. Byrd said."

"So that means we're in charge," Sherman said.

Zac stood up a little straighter then, like he liked that idea, so I quickly added, "Plus, all of the campers are in elementary school, so they'll look up to us because we're older."

Before Zac could say anything else, I grabbed my clipboard. "So we were talking about some of the activities we'll be doing with the campers."

"Wait!" Tally interrupted. "Who put you in charge of this, anyway? You're a seventh grader."

I started to tell her that I wasn't exactly "in charge," but Baylor jumped in and said, "This meeting was Morgan's idea, so she should lead it. Just listen, okay?"

Tally still didn't look too happy, but she didn't say anything else, either.

So I went on. "Like I was saying, Monday's activity is called Musical Petting Zoo."

Davis laughed. "A musical petting zoo? I've never heard of that."

"*Oui!*" Lem agreed. "Are the campers going to play music for some goats and ponies?"

Colby grabbed his pretend instrument and played air saxophone, while Sherman joined in on his invisible flute.

Zac couldn't resist getting in on the performance. "Baaa!" he bleated like a goat.

"Neigh!" Davis did his best horse impression.

By then, everyone was dying laughing. I should've called our meeting back to order, but even I couldn't pass up this much fun. Baylor joined me for an air clarinet duet. Carmen played a beat on her invisible drum. And Hope threw in a "Hee-haw! Hee-haw!"

Just then, the grounds keeper walked by with clippers to weed the flower bed.

"Hello, Mr. Harvey!" Tally waved.

Mr. Harvey waved back. Then he took off his glasses, wiped them on the hem of his shirt, and slid them back on.

"Look, he thinks he's seeing things!" Zac laughed.

Of course, that made us all laugh even harder.

Mr. Harvey shook his head. When he walked away, he mumbled, "Kids these days."

"Okay," I said, holding my stomach from laughing so hard. "We really need to get back on track here. I'm pretty sure there won't be any farm animals, since camp is going to be inside." Then I held up the flyer. "It says, 'Come join in the fun as we take a rollicking romp through the musical petting zoo.'"

"Seriously," Miles said, wheeling forward in his wheelchair, "what is a musical petting zoo?"

I shrugged. "I think it'll be like a petting zoo at a farm. Only instead of animals, there'll be lots of musical instruments for the kids to see and touch."

"No way!" Kori said. "Those kids aren't petting Russell."

Now I was really confused. "Who's Russell?"

"Russell is my trombone," Kori explained. "And no, it's not weird that he has a name."

I shook my head. "Nope. Lots of people name their instruments."

"They're not getting their sticky little hands on my flute either," Sherman said.

"Eight- and nine-year-olds aren't usually sticky," I said. "It's five-year-olds you've got to look out for. Trust me. My little brother is in kindergarten."

Sherman didn't care. "It doesn't matter if the campers are five, nine, ten, or twenty plus ten. No one's going to touch my flute except me," he said.

"Maybe we should talk about Tuesday's activity," I suggested. "It's called Human Musical Notes."

"What's that about?" Hope asked, peering over my shoulder.

I flipped the flyer over and read, "What do people and musical scales have in common? Absolutely nothing! Until now, that is. In an exercise of Human Musical Notes, humans and music notes collide."

"That sounds interesting, *mademoiselle*," Lem said.

So I kept going and told everyone about Wednesday's musical scavenger hunt. There were tons of games planned throughout the week, too, like musical chairs and rhythm relays. And there was a treble clef spelling bee, using only the letters of music notes to spell out different words.

"Basically," Zac interrupted, "it sounds like we'll be babysitters at this camp. And I'm not so great with little kids."

I ignored him and kept going. "Camp officially ends on Friday with Family Night."

"What's that about?" Miles asked.

"That's when all of the campers' families get to come to the community center to see what the kids have worked on all week," I explained. "The art campers will display their masterpieces, the theater kids will put on a skit, and the ones who enrolled in the music camp will play songs for their families."

"Wow! If their families are coming, this is a big deal," Sherman said.

"Right," I agreed. "So it has to be perfect."

Baylor smiled. "We all know the clarinet section will be amazing."

"Are you kidding me?" Zac asked. "The sax section will blow the clarinets right out of the water. Ka-boom!"

"Don't count on it, Zac," Baylor shot back. "Right, Morgan?"

I didn't exactly want to get in the middle of this. But Baylor nudged me and said "Right?" again, so I sort of didn't have a choice.

"Right," I said, a little more confidently than I felt.

Zac grinned. "Hey, don't say I didn't warn you."

I wasn't too worried about it. Two things I was good at were playing clarinet and keeping little kids in line. This camp would be a piece of cake.

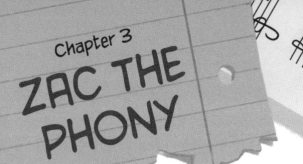

Chapter 3

ZAC THE PHONY

"Good morning, everyone!" Mr. Byrd said early Monday morning. "Are you ready for our first day of camp?"

"*Oui, monsieur!*" Lem said.

I smiled. "I can't wait to meet the campers."

"Excellent!" Mr. Byrd smiled, too. "The campers are already being seated in the auditorium for announcements, so we'll head in there, as well. Follow me!"

So all of us got settled into our seats. A few minutes later, a lady stepped up on the stage. The microphone was seriously taller than she was, and she adjusted it down to her level before she spoke. "Hello, boys and girls! My name is Mrs. Harman, and I am the director of Benton Bluff's Summer

Arts Camp. On behalf of everyone here, welcome to camp!"

The auditorium erupted in a round of applause.

"Thank you!" Mrs. Harman said. "Now, raise your hand if this is your first year to attend our day camp."

Hands shot up all across the room.

Mrs. Harman nodded. "Well, you're certainly in for quite a treat." She paused before continuing with, "If you're signed up for art camp, it's going to get messy. If you're enrolled in our theater camp, there'll be lots of drama. And if you're one of our musician campers, this week will be filled with plenty of high notes."

Davis drummed his fingers on the back of the chair in front of him at that joke. "Bah-dum-ch!"

"That's so corny," Zac whispered, kicking back in his seat.

Mr. Byrd shot them both a look, and they cut it out.

After that, Mrs. Harman went over the week's schedule and added that without volunteers to lead the campers, none of this would be possible. "Without further ado," Mrs. Harman went on, "let me introduce our camp leaders."

She called up each leader, one by one. First was the art instructor, who looked old enough to be Picasso's teacher. Next, the theater instructor, who looked like a biker dude. No joke! And then Mrs. Harman called Mr. Byrd's name.

"Go, Mr. Byrd!" Sherman shouted. All of us band members clapped extra hard. And Zac and Colby even pumped their fists in the air.

"We're looking forward to a great week," Mrs. Harman said when the applause died down. "At this time, we'll dismiss into our different groups."

So the rest of the band members and I followed Mr. Byrd back to our classroom. Someone had spent a lot of time decorating the room in a cool jungle theme. Cardboard gorillas swung from music notes hanging from the ceiling. There were even pots of artificial trees with big tropical leaves and brightly colored birds perched on the limbs. It was impressive.

First, Mr. Byrd took roll and introduced us band kids to the group. Then he asked, "How many of you have been to a petting zoo before?"

Nearly every hand waved in the air. "I have!" one of the girls said. "I got to pet every animal there."

Mr. Byrd smiled. "That's right! At a petting zoo, you get to pet all of the animals, and you learn how they're alike and how they're different. For example, a pony has a smooth coat while a goat's coat is coarse."

"And a pony is bigger," a boy pointed out.

"But they both can live on a farm," another kid pointed out.

"Exactly!" Mr. Byrd nodded. "Just like animals, musical instruments are alike in some ways and very different in others." He walked over to the instruments arranged on tables in the center of the room and held up a trumpet and a trombone. "How are these two instruments alike?"

"They're both shiny!" a kid shouted.

"Their names both start with a *t*," another boy said.

Mr. Byrd nodded again. "And they're both members of the same family, called the brass family." He walked around showing the kids the mouthpieces and telling them how a musician made sound by buzzing his lips.

When Mr. Byrd put the brass instruments back on the table, he held up a clarinet and a saxophone. "What do you notice about these two instruments?"

"I notice that one's cool, and the other one isn't," Zac whispered.

All of us who heard him knew he meant that the sax was cooler since that's what he played.

"Yeah, the clarinet is way cooler than the sax," I whispered back.

Zac frowned.

One of the girls raised her hand to answer Mr. Byrd's question. "They're different colors."

"And shapes, too," Mr. Byrd said. "But check out their mouthpieces. These instruments belong to the woodwind family, and their sound is made by using a reed."

Mr. Byrd placed those instruments back on the table, too. When he'd talked about the flute, the snare drum, and the French horn, Mr. Byrd said, "Now it's time for some fun. Head over to our musical petting zoo where you can explore the different instruments. It's a chance to check out an instrument you don't already play. If you have any questions, ask me or one of my students for help."

All of the kids rushed to the tables. They picked up the instruments and checked out their tubes and bells and keys.

Sherman cringed when one of the kids nearly dropped a flute. "I am so glad the community center provided the instruments, so we didn't have to use ours," he said.

"Me too!" Kori agreed.

After a while, one of the campers noticed the decorations. "Look at that snake!" He pointed to this giant stuffed boa constrictor draped above a window.

"Don't let it bite you!" Zac said, making a hissing sound.

The kid screamed, and Zac laughed.

"Zac!" I frowned. "Don't scare him."

"Hey, he knows I'm joking. Don't you, buddy?" Zac said to him.

When the kid nodded, Zac held his hand out for a high five.

"See?" Zac said. "We're just goofing off. Besides, Sam here knows boa constrictors don't have a poisonous bite, right? They squeeze their prey."

Zac grabbed the boa constrictor and draped it around Sam's shoulders.

"How'd you know his name?" one of the girls asked.

"Because, um," Zac stuttered before saying, "I know everything."

The girl smiled and said, "Nuh-uh!"

Zac grinned. "Nah, I don't know everything. But I do know how to read name tags, and it says Sam right there on his. And yours says Tatum."

Some other kids had gathered around. "What's my name tag say?" another girl asked, trying to hide hers with her hand so Zac couldn't read it.

"Too late!" Zac grinned. "I've already read your name tag. It says Aliyah."

Aliyah laughed.

"And your name tag says Lincoln," Zac went on. "Yours says Julie Ann. And yours says Matt."

Matt reached for the stuffed snake, still wound around Sam's shoulders, and wrapped Zac up in

it. All of the kids laughed when Zac made a big show of modeling in it, like it was one of those fluffy feather boas.

"You're funny!" Julie Ann said.

"You think so?" Zac asked, whirling around like some runway supermodel.

I reached for the snake and said, "That's enough, Zac. We're supposed to help with the petting zoo activity, not play with the props."

"Morgan's no fun, is she?" Zac said to the kids.

Then Zac pretended that the snake's big, pink forked tongue was striking at me. And the kids clapped, like we were putting on a show.

"This isn't theater camp," I reminded Zac and took the snake away from him. "So this guy is going back to the window where he belongs." Only, no matter how high I stretched on my tiptoes, I still couldn't put that stuffed boa back above the window where Zac had gotten it in the first place.

The kids laughed even more.

"All right, campers, we're ready for our next activity," Mr. Byrd said then. "That is, if we can get Morgan to stop playing with the stuffed animals."

"But I wasn't—" I started to tell Mr. Byrd that I wasn't the one who was playing around. This whole thing was Zac's fault.

I didn't have a chance, though, because Zac jumped up and took the snake from me and put it back above the window himself.

"Thank you, Zac!" Mr. Byrd said.

"You're welcome, sir," Zac said. Then he had the nerve to look at me and flash me this innocent smile, like he hadn't done anything wrong.

The kids looked at Zac like he was some kind of superhero. Seriously!

I was starting to think Zac was a big phony. He'd said he wasn't good with younger kids. What a lie! So far, all of the campers loved him.

Chapter 4
SAXES VS. CLARINETS

After a game of musical chairs, Mr. Byrd said, "Campers, for our next activity, we'll form smaller groups by instrument for music lessons. My Benton Bluff band students will lead you in this exercise, and I'll come around to oversee the progress of each group."

"I want to be in Zac's group!" Sam said, smiling.

"Zac is leading the saxophone section, Sam," Mr. Byrd said. "Do you play sax?"

Sam shook his head.

Mr. Byrd said, "You play clarinet, right? Baylor and Morgan are leading that section."

"But I don't want to be in their group," Sam grumbled.

"It'll be great. Please join us, Sam," I said.

Baylor held out her hand to Sam and said, "Come with us. We're learning a cool new song."

Sam shook his head and held on to his seat.

It was sort of embarrassing that Sam wouldn't cooperate. Everyone watched to see what would happen next. It was like a showdown. And Sam wasn't budging.

"Come on," I said a little more forcefully. That tone of voice always worked with my little brother.

When Sam still didn't get up, I shot my co-counselor Baylor a look, silently pleading. *A little help here!*

Instead of Baylor helping, Zac did. He leaned down and whispered something in Sam's ear.

Whatever Zac said to him worked because Sam came over and grabbed my hand. "Let's go!" he said.

I was super surprised. First, I couldn't believe Zac had jumped in to help our group. And second, I couldn't believe Sam actually listened to him.

By now, Sam was tugging on my hand. But I managed to say, "Thanks, Zac!" before we headed over for clarinet practice.

"You're welcome." Zac grinned.

Each of the musical sections was divided into different areas of the room. Our group was in a corner near a window.

"What do we do now?" Baylor whispered.

"Don't worry. Mr. Byrd gave us some instructions." I pointed to my clipboard. "I have everything right here."

Baylor looked relieved. "Good! Because I'm not that good with younger kids."

Zac had said the same thing, and it wasn't true. At all. So Baylor was probably exaggerating, too.

But just in case, I took the lead. "Let me make sure we have everyone here who signed up for our group. When I call your name, please raise your hand." I glanced at my clipboard and called, "Aliyah. Connor. Tatum. Mischa. And Sam."

One by one, each camper raised his or her hand. Except Sam.

"Please raise your hand, Sam," I said.

"Why? You already know I'm here."

I nodded. "You're right. But I asked you to raise your hand. If you don't, then you're not following directions."

"So?" Sam said.

"So," I answered, "to be a great musician, you have to follow directions. If you don't raise your hand when someone asks you to, how can you follow directions to play the notes on your music?"

Baylor looked impressed by that explanation. "That's good!" she said.

"Thanks!" I smiled.

But Sam wasn't smiling. "I don't feel like raising my hand. What are you going to do about it?"

Actually, there were a couple of things I wanted to do just then. One involved calling Sam a brat, which is what I'd normally do if my little brother acted like that. The other involved trading Sam for a different camper.

But since I couldn't do either of those things, I decided to pretend that this corner of the classroom was the Carnegie Hall stage and I was a professional conductor. So I plastered on a smile and ignored the way Sam was acting.

"Moving on!" I said extra happily. "All of you play clarinet at your schools, right?"

When everyone nodded, I said, "Awesome! So you all know how to assemble your instruments. Please do that now."

Mr. Byrd came over to our group. "How's it going, girls?"

"Great!" I lied, er, said. "We're about to start practicing our first song."

"That's what I like to hear! I'll be back around to check on your section in a few minutes." Mr. Byrd flashed us a thumbs-up before taking off to the next group.

"Mr. Byrd dresses funny," Sam said, laughing.

I frowned. "Don't say that. It's not nice."

"Neither are you," Sam shot back.

For half a second, I almost stuck my tongue out at him and mimicked him with, "Neither are you!"

But professional, future Carnegie Hall conductor me took over again. "Does anyone need any help assembling your instrument?" I asked.

"Mine's together," Aliyah said. She blew into her mouthpiece to prove it. It sounded like a screeching goose.

"Okay, that's good," I said, flipping over to the sheet music clipped to my board. "We have two songs to work on this week. One is called 'Pink Popsicles.' The other is 'The Llama's Grand Mama.'"

Tatum giggled. "Those names are silly."

"They are sort of silly," I agreed, passing out the sheet music to everyone. "But by the end of the week, you're going to play these songs so well that they'll sound amazing."

"Yeah," Baylor chimed in. "Your families will love hearing you play at Family Night on Friday."

I nodded. "That's right. But first, we have to practice. So let's begin with 'Pink Popsicles.'"

Before we actually played the song, I pointed out the meter. "There are four beats per measure." Then I reviewed the note lengths with the campers. "Hold a whole note for four counts, a half note for two, and a quarter note for one. Got it?"

"Got it!" Connor said.

"Yeah, we're not babies," Sam added.

"No, you're not," I said. "But since it's summer break, I thought we could all use a quick refresher. Now let's talk about the notes in each measure. The first four notes are all quarter notes." I slid my clipboard beneath my arm and clapped as I counted them out.

We'd nearly counted to the last measure of the song when Mr. Byrd stopped by again. "Is everything still moving along nicely here?"

I nodded.

"Baylor, lead the group for a moment please while I talk to Morgan," Mr. Byrd said, pulling me over to the side. "Did Sam settle down once you got into your group?"

"Yes, sir," I said. "Honestly, he's been fine."

Okay, Sam hadn't been great. But I didn't want Mr. Byrd to know that. I wanted to prove he'd made the right decision choosing me as a counselor.

"Very good," Mr. Byrd said. "If any of the kids gives you and Baylor a hard time, let me know. We'll handle it accordingly."

I nodded. "Yes, sir."

Then I went back to our clarinet section. A few minutes later, Mr. Byrd clapped his hands. "Everyone, attention please! We only have ten minutes left in our sections before we move on to practicing in small ensembles."

Ten minutes! I glanced at my watch. I'd been so focused on teaching the basics that our section hadn't even practiced "Pink Popsicles" all the way through one time yet.

"As I've been checking in with different groups," Mr. Byrd continued, "I noticed one group was playing especially well. Everyone, take a moment to listen to our saxophone section." He pointed toward Colby and Zac. "Would you guys please share your group's progress with the rest of us?"

I could hardly believe it. I mean, Zac was such a goof-off. He'd even admitted he didn't want to be here at camp this week. So how was his section playing better than everyone else's?

I still hadn't forgotten what he'd said about the saxophone section blowing the clarinets out of the water. Apparently, Zac hadn't either.

Right before camp was over for the day, he came up to Baylor and me and bragged, "I told you the saxophone section would be better than the clarinets, didn't I?"

"We'll see about that!" I said.

Chapter 5
EARTH TO MORGAN

"I don't get it, Baylor," I said the next day. It was our second day of camp, and we'd just finished a game of rhythm relays outside on the lawn.

Baylor nodded. "I hear you. I thought our team was going to win that last race."

"No," I said. "I was talking about Zac, not the game."

"What's he done now?" Baylor sighed.

The way Baylor said it, I almost laughed. Everyone knew that Zac was sort of the band class clown. But then I remembered how Mr. Byrd recognized the saxophone section for doing so great at our first practice, and not the clarinets. This was definitely nothing to laugh at.

"I just don't get how the saxophone section played so well yesterday," I went on. "I mean, how did Zac pull that off?"

"I've wondered the same thing." Baylor pulled me aside and looked around to make sure we were alone before whispering, "Have you noticed anything else strange about Zac?"

"Well," I began, "he does wear camouflage clothes all the time. That's pretty strange."

Baylor shook her head. "That's nothing new. I've known Zac practically my whole life. I'm pretty sure he showed up at preschool with a camouflage sippy cup."

Now I had to laugh. Picturing teeny tiny Zac toddling around with a sippy cup was funny.

"I'm not kidding," Baylor said, smiling too. "But seriously, have you noticed anything, let's just say, unusual, about Zac?"

I thought about it. "Now that you mention it, what about yesterday when Sam was supposed to join us in the clarinet section. Nobody else could get him to cooperate," I said. "Not Mr. Byrd. Not me. But Sam listened to Zac."

"I noticed that, too." Baylor's voice got real serious then. "Zac is up to something fishy."

"He does talk about fishing a lot," I pointed out.

Baylor shook her head. "No, I mean, he's up to something fishy. As in, no good. And we have to figure out what that is."

"We?" I squeaked.

"You got it," Baylor said, pointing to me and then to herself. "We're on the case."

"I'm not so sure about this," I began. Baylor was a school newspaper reporter. She was used to tracking down a story, but I wasn't. Besides, mysteries were always my least favorite stories to read. They seemed sort of hokey to me. "I don't know anything about detective-ing."

Baylor smiled. "I don't think *detective-ing* is a word, Morgan."

"See? Point proven. I stink at this already."

"There's nothing to it, really. Just act natural. But be observant. And ask questions that will give you clues to solve the mystery," Baylor explained.

"You make it sound easy," I said.

"It is!" Baylor promised. Then she linked her arm through mine and said, "Let's go!"

I dug in my heels. "Wait! Where are we going?"

"To investigate Zac, silly," Baylor said, never slowing down.

Finding Zac was easy. There was a crowd of campers gathered around in a circle, and Zac, Davis, and Sherman were right in the middle of them all. But talking to Zac, that was a little harder.

"How are we supposed to find out anything?" I asked.

Baylor put one finger up to her lips to shush me. "Observe," she whispered.

I tried to. But I didn't observe anything suspicious. Sherman showed off some cool yo-yo tricks to the campers. Davis and Zac just sort of hung out watching Sherman, too.

"I don't see the big deal," I said. "Everything seems totally normal to me."

"Where's Sam?" Baylor asked.

Had she lost it? Anybody could plainly see Sam standing beside Zac. But I played along and pointed him out. "He's right there."

"Exactly!" Baylor said. "Isn't it weird that Sam likes Zac so much? They just met yesterday, but it's almost like they already knew each other."

"You got all of that from observing Zac and Sam hanging out and watching Sherman do his walk the dog yo-yo trick?" No wonder I didn't like mysteries. You had to practically be a genius to figure them out.

"It could be a clue." Baylor pointed to her brain and said, "I'll file away that information for later."

It was a good thing, because Mr. Byrd came over then and said, "Listen up, campers! The last activity we have scheduled before lunch is our small ensemble groups. That means all of the brass sections will practice together, and our woodwind sections will also practice together."

"You know what else that means?" Baylor said as we followed Mr. Byrd back inside.

I shook my head.

"It's the perfect time for us to talk to Zac." She wiggled her eyebrows up and down.

It still wasn't that easy, though. Once we were in the classroom, Mr. Byrd went over some things. First, he taught some breathing exercises.

"Pretend your lungs have a top half and a bottom half. Filling up the top half is pretty easy. But take nice, deep breaths to fill the bottom half, too. Like filling a soda bottle from the bottom to the top," Mr. Byrd demonstrated and asked the campers to stand up to practice taking deep breaths.

Mischa and Tatum giggled until I told them to cut it out. I wished they'd take band more seriously.

Maybe they would after having me as a counselor all week.

"Next, assemble your instruments, and we'll practice long tones," Mr. Byrd continued.

"That's boring," Connor said. "Why can't we just play a real song?"

Mr. Byrd smiled. "We'll get to that, Connor. But before playing a 'real song,' as you call it, it's important to fill your technique toolbox with multiple teaching tools. Long tones not only help with breath control, they also improve your endurance." He turned toward us junior high kids. "Just ask my school band members."

"That's true," Hope spoke up. "I thought practicing long tones was kind of boring, too. But I promise, it really does help give you enough air to play longer songs."

After practicing some long tones, lip slurs, and tonguing techniques, Mr. Byrd finally broke us into two smaller groups. The trumpet, trombone, and

French horn players went to one side of the room. Even though that group was the brass family, the percussion players joined them, too. And the flute, saxophone, and clarinet players went to the other side to form the woodwind family.

"Counselors, please have your groups practice 'Pink Popsicles,'" Mr. Byrd said. "While you give the kids one-on-one instruction, I'll flip-flop between the two groups."

Sherman took over our group, and Baylor whispered, "Here's our chance to finally ask Zac some questions to find out what he's up to. Just act natural."

I nodded and whispered back, "Act natural. Got it!"

"Hey, Zac!" Baylor said, heading toward him.

"What's up?" he asked.

Baylor twisted her long, black braid. "Not much." Then she looked at me like I should say something.

But now that Zac stood in front of me, I didn't actually know what to say. I just sort of stared at him, like a giant goober. Then a few questions popped into my mind. Like, why haven't I ever noticed that dimple in your left cheek before? Or, has anyone ever told you that your eyes are stormy sky blue? And, why did I just notice that you're kind of cute? Okay, that was all pretty weird.

"Hello!" Zac waved his hand in front of my face then. "Earth to Morgan. Do you read me, Morgan?" He talked in this weird voice, like he was mission

control contacting an astronaut. All of the kids around us started cracking up.

Something happened then. Because instead of acting natural and all smooth like Baylor suggested, I blurted out, "So what did you say to Sam yesterday to get him to join my group when Mr. Byrd and I couldn't get him to budge?"

Zac grinned. "Magic!"

"Too bad I don't believe in magic," I said.

"Well you should." Zac leaned in closer and pretended to pull something from behind my ear.

When he opened his hand, a shiny quarter rested in his palm. He held it up for all of the campers in our group to see. They all clapped, like it was the most amazing trick ever. And Zac took a bow, like he was the greatest magician ever.

"Do you believe in magic now?" Zac asked.

I shook my head. "Nope. Magic just tricks an audience into believing they're seeing something that they're really not. It's all fake."

It was sort of like that with Zac, too. Everyone knew he was a goof-off. And now he was suddenly the perfect camp counselor, impressing Mr. Byrd and all of the kids.

Which was the real Zac, and which was the phony? It was up to Baylor and me to reveal his secrets.

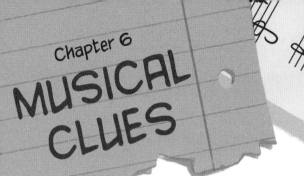

Chapter 6

MUSICAL CLUES

"Zac, can I talk to you in private for a moment please?" Mr. Byrd said the next morning before the campers arrived in the classroom.

Baylor and I looked at each other. "I wonder what that's about," I whispered.

Baylor shrugged. "I'm sure we'll find out later."

I shook my head. "I don't know. I mean, our detective-ing yesterday didn't go so great."

"That's totally okay, though," Baylor assured me. "Cracking a case takes time."

Then I got a great idea. "I know! Maybe we should talk to some of the kids in Zac's group."

"That's perfect!" Baylor smiled. "See, you're already thinking like a detective."

Just then, Lincoln came into the classroom.

Baylor and I went over to say hi and to see what he might tell us about Zac.

"How's camp going, Lincoln?" Baylor asked.

"Fine, I guess," he said.

"Only fine?" I said. "The saxophone section did so great the first day of camp that Mr. Byrd asked you guys to play for everyone."

Lincoln nodded. "But we already knew how to play 'Pink Popsicles.'"

"What do you mean you already knew how to play it?" Baylor asked.

"I mean, Mr. DiMeo already taught us that song," Lincoln said.

Now I was confused. "Wait, who's Mr. DiMeo?"

"Mr. DiMeo is the band director at my school," Lincoln explained. "Malone Elementary."

"Do all of you saxophone players go to the same school?" Baylor asked.

Lincoln nodded. "Yep."

"Wow!" I looked at Baylor. This was big news.

Baylor knew it, too. She leaned over and whispered, "You know what that means, Morgan?"

I knew exactly what it meant. Mr. DiMeo was the sax players' band director. He'd already taught them to play "Pink Popsicles." That meant the "progress" Mr. Byrd said the sax section made on Monday was all thanks to Mr. DiMeo. Not Zac.

Lincoln frowned. "What's the big deal?"

"We're just surprised, that's all," Baylor said.

"Yeah, thanks for telling us all of this, Lincoln," I said.

He shrugged. "You're welcome, I guess." Then Matt and Sam waved at him. When Lincoln took off toward them, I heard him say, "Girls are so weird."

And that was the end of our detective-ing for a while. Because by then, Mr. Byrd and Zac had returned to the classroom.

"Today, our first activity is a musical scavenger hunt," Mr. Byrd announced. "Counselors, you'll work together with your section to find everything on this list. Once you find an item, snap a photo on your phone. The first section to finish wins."

"What do we win?" Matt asked.

Mr. Byrd smiled. "Bragging rights."

Julie Ann stuck out her tongue. "I was hoping for a prize," she said as each group grabbed a list.

Then Mr. Byrd yelled, "Go!"

"What's the first thing on our list?" Sam asked.

"Why don't you tell me?" I turned the sheet around so Sam could see it.

"Number one," he read, "I have lost of keys."

Aliyah scrunched up her nose and repeated, "'Lost of keys.' What's that mean?"

The clue totally didn't make any sense to me either. I took a closer look. "Oh! It says *lots* of keys. Not *lost* of keys."

When some of the kids laughed, Sam's cheeks turned pink.

"It's no big deal," I said, changing the subject back to our scavenger hunt.

"But what's something in this classroom with lots of keys?" Baylor added.

"We could see if Mr. Byrd has a key chain," Connor suggested. "My dad's has tons of keys."

Tatum shook her head. "It has to be something musical."

"Right," Connor said.

"Look all around," I said, pointing in different directions. "Do you see anything, Sam?"

He shook his head, but he wouldn't look at me. And he wouldn't look for an object to solve the clue, either. He seemed mad for some reason.

"Are you okay?" I asked him.

He didn't have time to answer because Mischa shouted, "Hey, a piano has lots of keys!"

"That's gotta be it," Baylor said.

So we had our group gather around the piano while I snapped a picture of them with my phone.

"Can I read the next clue?" Aliyah asked. "I'm a good reader." She looked at Sam when she said it.

"Sure," I said, handing her our list. "But if we're going to win, we'd better hurry."

"Number two: Notes rest on me," Aliyah said.

Tatum pointed to the whiteboard near the front of the room. "Easy! A staff."

"I think you've got it," I said, taking a picture of the kids with the staff Mr. Byrd had drawn on the board with a green marker.

We went around the room and found nearly everything on our list. "Last clue," Baylor said. "At Thanksgiving, you might fight over me."

"Pumpkin pie!" Connor said, licking his lips.

Mischa put her hands on her hips. "Does your family eat musical pumpkin pie?"

"Well," Connor said, thinking, "when my grandpa burps after eating dessert, it does sort of sound like a musical performance, I guess."

"Eww!" the rest of the campers said together.

"Okay, that's enough," I said, trying to focus their attention back on our scavenger hunt. I really wanted our group to win. That would probably impress Mr. Byrd and everyone else, too. "Think about the main course on your Thanksgiving dinner table."

"Ham?" Tatum guessed.

I shook my head. "Some people do have ham, but most people have—" To give them a hint, I flapped my arms up and down.

"Most people have turkey," Aliyah said.

"Right!" I smiled.

"So what's a part of the turkey that you might fight over that's musical?" Baylor asked.

Sam was still way more quiet than usual. "Any guesses, Sam?" I asked.

"Nope," he said. I could tell he wasn't even trying to think of an answer.

"I know!" Connor said. "It's a drumstick!"

Baylor held up her hand for a high five. "You got it!"

"Let's get a picture of you guys with a couple of drumsticks," I said, posing them beside a snare.

As soon as I snapped the picture, we hurried over to Mr. Byrd. We were almost there, too, when Sherman and Hope's group ran up to Mr. Byrd first.

After Mr. Byrd checked out Hope's cell phone pictures, he said, "We have a winner, folks! Let's give the flute section a round of applause."

"That stinks," Aliyah said. "We almost won."

"It's okay!" I said. But really, I wasn't so sure it was okay. I mean, so far our group had bombed every game we played. Making this section look good definitely wasn't easy, but I added, "We'll try harder next time."

Sam mumbled, "Next time, I hope I'm in Zac's group."

"But Zac's group didn't win the scavenger hunt either, Sam," I said.

He shrugged. "You don't get it."

Sam was right. I didn't get it. But I wanted to. I was pretty sure Zac got whatever was going on with Sam. That's why Baylor and I had to figure out what the deal was with those two.

"If you tell me what's going on, I might understand," I said softly.

Sam looked at me. For a second, I thought maybe he might open up to me. Like, maybe tell me why he got so upset during the scavenger hunt.

But then he mumbled, "Just forget it."

I had to. For now, at least. Because Mr. Byrd announced, "It's time for individual sections to practice. Today, we'll play a new song called, 'The Llama's Grand Mama.' Counselors, please have your campers assemble their instruments."

"C'mon, guys!" I said to my group. "I hope you like this song."

And I hoped our clarinet section would excel at playing it and even get recognized for our hard work. Yesterday, Mr. Byrd praised Lem and Miles for their progress with the trumpet section.

I still had to prove to Mr. Byrd that I was a great camp counselor. And prove to myself that I had what it took to make it as a big-time conductor.

To make that happen, this clarinet section was going to have to practice extra hard. Starting now!

Chapter 7
CLIPBOARD RESCUE

"We only have two days of camp left, guys," I said, reaching for my clipboard. "And you really want to wow your families on Friday at Family Night, don't you?"

Aliyah and Connor both nodded.

"Then we have to stop playing around and practice super hard," I said.

"But we have been practicing super hard," Mischa said.

I smiled. "We have, but now it's time to practice *extra* super hard." It was true. I wanted our clarinet section to wow their families at Family Night. But I also wanted to wow Mr. Byrd. Maybe even more.

And besides, if I couldn't get a bunch of elementary school students to create amazing music, how could I ever be a famous Carnegie Hall conductor someday? My whole future career could be in trouble here if the campers blew this.

"Take out your sheet music," I said, not wasting another second.

"The Llama's Grand Mama," Tatum said, placing her music on the stand in front of her. "Say that three times fast."

"We don't have time for goofing off right now," I said. "Everyone, please look at the first measure." We scanned through every note and every rest in the entire song, from the first measure all the way to the last.

Mischa's hand shot up.

"Not now, Mischa," I said.

"But it's really important," Mischa said.

"It can wait until later. Okay?"

Mr. Byrd was headed in our direction, and I really wanted him to notice my leadership skills.

"On my count," I said. "One and two and ready

and play!" I gave it everything I had, waving my hands up and down, leading the campers through each measure. I was pretty sure the llama's mama had never been more grand than when I was conducting that song just then.

The look on Mr. Byrd's face as he watched wasn't so grand, though. Honestly, he looked pretty freaked out. And then he yelled, "Stop!"

I couldn't stop, though. The song's tempo was allegro. That meant really fast. And my hands were flying at allegro speed, too. There was no stopping them, even if I wanted to. Out of the corner of my eye, I could see people all across the room turning to watch me conduct my section. This was my moment to shine, and I was.

Then suddenly, everything happened in a blur. Mr. Byrd sprang toward me and took off his straw hat, wildly waving it back and forth. Mischa shouted, "Spider!" And all of the kids in my group started screaming.

I looked up, and there it was, dangling by a silky thread right above my head. Its green arachnid eyes stared straight into mine.

"Kill it!" Sherman shouted, grabbing Mr. Byrd's hat right out of his hand.

"Not with my favorite hat!" Mr. Byrd said.

Zac ran over then and grabbed my clipboard. "I've got this," he said.

"My clipboard!" I cried. Zac was two seconds from squishing spider guts all over it. I couldn't stand to watch. So I covered my eyes.

But when everybody clapped, I couldn't resist taking a peek. And I couldn't believe what I saw. Instead of smashed goo, the spider crawled around on my clipboard. It was alive and well.

"It's not poisonous," Zac said. "I'll take Mr. Spider outside so he can find a new home."

Mr. Byrd nodded and fanned himself with his sheet music. "Yes, you do that, Zac. And everyone else, please continue on with your practice."

My group returned to their seats then.

"Thanks a lot for telling me about that spider, guys," I said.

Mischa looked annoyed. "I tried telling you, but you said it could wait until later."

She was right. Mischa had even told me it was important. I was just too focused on practicing our song to listen to her.

"I must've looked like a real goober, huh?" I said, hoping the kids would tell me I didn't look as silly as I felt.

"Yep, you sure did," Tatum said.

Sam laughed. "You looked like this." He did an impression of me flailing my arms around, like I was doing the wave or something. "And then you yelled, 'My clipboard!'"

The other kids started laughing, too.

Somehow, Baylor managed to keep a straight face when she said, "Don't worry, Morgan. You didn't look that bad."

Here I was trying to impress Mr. Byrd. Instead, I'd looked super dumb. Practice had turned into a major musical disaster.

"Never mind," I said. "Let's just start over. Take it from the top!"

Even when all of the other sections took a short break, I had my group keep practicing. After individual sections practiced, Mr. Byrd moved us right into small ensemble practice. Then it was time for lunch.

I got a great idea. "We could practice straight through lunch today," I told my group.

"No way!" Connor said.

"So what if you eat really fast? That way we can still squeeze in a few more minutes of practice during our lunch break," I bargained, hoping they'd be willing to compromise.

"Not happening!" Tatum said. "A bunch of us pretend like we're royalty after we eat. And today, it's my turn to be queen."

I smiled. "That's cool. But if we practice instead, then for the rest of the day, your official title can be Queen Tatum, Fair Ruler of the Clarinet."

Tatum shook her head and took off for the cafeteria with the rest of the group

"Give it up, Morgan," Baylor said. "They're not buying it."

So as soon as lunch was over, everyone met back in the classroom.

"We'll begin music theory with a flash card game," Mr. Byrd began. He held up cards, and the campers guessed the correct name of the musical symbols. Like a quarter rest that sort of looked like a lighting bolt. And a fermata, which meant hold. The dot reminded me of an eye, and the curve above it looked like a creepy eyebrow.

While they played their game, I decided to check the schedule to see what activity was planned next. There was only one problem. I couldn't find my clipboard. I searched under the seats, behind the instrument cases, and on top of the piano. Still nothing.

"What are you looking for?" Baylor asked.

"My clipboard," I said. "Have you seen it?"

Baylor shook her head. "I think you had it at lunch."

"No, I didn't have it then either."

"Stop and think about it the last place you remember seeing it," Baylor suggested.

I remembered bringing it to camp this morning. And I had it with me during section practice before lunch. "That's it!" I snapped my fingers. "Zac used it to transport that spider to his new home outside. He never gave it back."

As soon as I got a chance, I went right up to Zac and held out my hand. "Hand it over!"

"Here you go!" He grinned and gave me five.

That was super annoying, but I kept my cool. "Very funny, Zac," I said. "But you know exactly what I'm talking about."

Zac looked confused. "No, really, I don't. Why don't you tell me?"

I almost believed him. Except, you know, Zac had it last. I'd seen him with my own eyes and everything. "My clipboard," I finally said. "Give it back."

"Oh, that!" Zac said. "I already gave it back."

"Where'd you put it then?"

"Over there by the window." He pointed to the corner where the clarinet section practiced.

"But it's not there now," I said. "And I've looked everywhere for it."

Zac shrugged. "How could it just disappear?"

I thought about Zac's magic trick. He made that quarter appear from behind my ear. If he could do that, I bet he could make things disappear, too.

"Okay," I said. "The joke's over. Give my clipboard back, Zac."

"That's where I left it. No kidding," he insisted.

I guessed he could tell I still didn't buy it.

"Hey, this is like the last band camp all over again. I didn't take anyone's instruments then, and I didn't take your clipboard now," Zac said.

"Then who did?" I asked.

"Beats me," Zac said. "But I'll help you look around for it."

He did. And so did Baylor and Hope and Lem. It was sort of like yesterday's scavenger hunt. Except nobody won. Because no matter how hard we looked, we never found my clipboard.

Chapter 8

SPELLING BEE BLUES

On Thursday morning, I showed up at camp early before the campers arrived to look for my clipboard again. But by the time the other counselors showed up, still no luck.

"It's okay, *mademoiselle*," Lem said. "I'm sure it will turn up."

"I hope so," I said.

"It's just a dumb clipboard," Zac said. "What's the big deal, anyway?"

The big deal was that I was sort of lost without it. I mean, to most people it was "a dumb clipboard," like Zac said. But it kept me organized. I checked it over and over again all day long to make sure I stayed on track. I had to get it back. Lem and Zac and the others wouldn't understand.

Wait a sec! That reminded me of Sam. He'd told me I didn't get why he wanted to be in Zac's group so bad after our scavenger hunt. Now I was convinced more than ever that something was going on with him. Something big. I had to talk to Baylor.

"I hope everyone is ready for today's first activity, Music Note Spelling Bee," Mr. Byrd said then, drawing a music staff on the board.

Some of the campers clapped.

"An easy way to remember the names of the notes that go on the lines is by remembering the phrase Every Good Boy Does Fine." Mr. Byrd said the name of each note as he drew it on the right line. "Now, does anyone know the phrase to help you remember the names of the notes in the spaces?"

I whispered to my section, "C'mon, guys. Tell Mr. Byrd the answer." They had to know the right answer. I'd gone over the names of notes with them every day. And it would make me look like a good counselor if someone from my group nailed this.

But Tatum yawned. And everyone else acted like they'd never even heard of a music note before.

"It's FACE," one of Kori and Ellen's trombone kids said. "F-A-C-E."

"Excellent!" Mr. Byrd smiled and wrote the names of the notes on the spaces, too.

I sighed and held my head in my hands. My group was killing me. It was almost like they purposefully tried to make me look bad in front of Mr. Byrd and everyone else, too.

Mr. Byrd held up circles with a different letter of a music note written on each one. "Everyone will take turns coming to the board and spelling out a different word using these music note letters only."

"Is it boys against girls?" Lincoln asked.

"Since it's worked well all week, let's stick with woodwinds versus brass," Mr. Byrd said. He also divided the percussion campers, putting half on each team.

The woodwinds went first. Lots of kids cheered when Julie Ann from Zac and Colby's saxophone section arranged the letters to spell out *CAFE*.

Even Mr. Byrd said, "That's quite impressive, Julie Ann!"

"Thanks!" She smiled and returned to our group.

The brass team came back with a good word, too, when one of the trumpet players spelled out *FADE*.

"Awesome, *monsieur*!" Lem said, holding up his hand for a high five.

Back and forth it went. Both teams came up with some great words. Some were five letters, like *CAGED*. And Raygan, one of the flutes, simply spelled the word *A* when it was her turn.

A few kids from the brass team grumbled about that one, but it still counted for our team!

"*A* is too a word," Raygan said. "As in, we're having *a* spelling bee."

Mr. Byrd pulled out a dictionary just to show us it was the first word listed. "Everyone can calm down now. Don't be upset that Raygan came up with a simple one you hadn't considered," he teased. "It's still worth a point!"

After a few more kids took turns spelling words, Mr. Byrd said, "We're nearly out of time, folks. If you haven't had an opportunity to spell a word, please raise your hand."

I leaned closer to Sam. "You haven't had a turn. Raise your hand."

He frowned. "Pass."

I started pointing at Sam, trying to get Mr. Byrd's attention so he'd call on him.

For some reason, Zac shook his head and motioned for me to cut it out. But it was too late.

"Sam, come on up front," Mr. Byrd said.

At first, I didn't think Sam was going to budge. It sort of reminded me of the very first day of camp when he refused to join our clarinet section. Thankfully, I wasn't in charge this time.

"Come on! I don't bite," Mr. Byrd insisted.

Almost in slow motion, Sam made his way toward the front of the room. He stared at the letters a few minutes before he even tried to arrange them to make a word. Once his hands finally moved, and he'd formed a word, he stood there frozen for a bit.

When he finally stepped away from the board, everyone could see his word. He'd spelled *DAB*. Only, there was one small problem. The *B* was reversed. At first, no one seemed to notice.

"Is dab a word?" one of the boys asked.

"Indeed it is," Mr. Byrd said. "It means a small amount. You might say, 'I'd like a dab of ketchup with my fries.'"

Then someone else pointed and said, "Look! Sam's *B* is backward." There was laughter.

"Thanks a lot, Morgan!" Sam said, storming out of the room.

Zac jumped up and took off right behind him.

"I'll go, too," I said. I mean, it was sort of my fault. I was the one who'd tried to get Mr. Byrd to call Sam up front. But I only did it so Sam would be involved. He'd seemed so quiet ever since the scavenger hunt.

At first, I didn't see Sam or Zac anywhere. They weren't in the hallway or in the lobby. Then I spotted them outside sitting on a bench.

"Sam," I said quietly, "I'm sorry that some of the kids laughed at you."

He glared at me. And his eyes were sort of puffy. I could tell he'd been crying.

"I was just trying to help," I continued. "I just wanted you to be a part of the team and have some fun, too."

"Fun? You think spelling is fun for me?" Sam exploded then. "Well, it isn't! And neither is reading. I hate them both! And I hate you, too, Morgan!"

Whoa! I seriously hadn't expected to hear that. And no lie, that stung. A lot!

"I promise I didn't mean to upset you, Sam." I looked at Zac, silently pleading for him to do something. Anything!

He didn't. And really, what did I expect him to do? I was the one who'd caused this whole mess. Not Zac.

"I'm sorry," I said again. "Please believe me."

"I don't believe you," he said. "All you care about is winning stuff and looking good in front of Mr. Byrd. You don't care about us."

Double ouch! That really hurt, too. I didn't say anything for a few minutes after that while I sat there thinking about everything Sam had said.

"You know, you're right," I finally said.

Sam looked surprised.

"This is my first year in a new band. The problem is, I've been so worried about making a good impression that I haven't been a very good counselor at all," I said. "I should've noticed the other day during the scavenger hunt when you read a clue and said *lost* instead of *lots*. You have dyslexia, right?"

Sam blinked. "You know about dyslexia?"

"Yeah," I said. "I know it makes people mix up letters sometimes when they're reading and spelling. That must stink, especially when other people laugh at you."

Sam nodded. "It does."

"I don't have dyslexia," I went on. "But I do sort of worry too much about stuff. I get frustrated when things aren't working right. I'm just really driven. It's no excuse or anything, but that's probably another reason I've pushed you guys so hard this week."

"See, Sam?" Zac jumped in then. "We all have stuff to deal with that's not so fun."

Sam seemed to think about it for a minute. Then he smiled and said, "Can I tell you guys a secret?"

"Sure," I said.

Zac nodded, too.

"I didn't mean to spell *dab* in there," Sam said. "I was trying to spell *bad*. I just got lucky that I spelled a real word." He even laughed a little.

Zac and I did, too.

"Don't worry," I said. "I'll never tell."

"Me neither," Zac promised.

Chapter 9

IN-SYNC SECTIONS

That afternoon, while the campers played on the playground after lunch, Mr. Byrd calling a surprise meeting for the counselors.

"I'd like to get your thoughts on how camp is going," he said. "Do you have any concerns? Or maybe have some tips for your fellow counselors that have helped your section this week?" He leaned against a tree. "Please share what's on your mind."

"The campers are cool," Davis spoke up. "It's been fun hanging out with them."

"Wonderful!" Mr. Byrd nodded. "Thank you, Davis. Anyone else?"

Hope went next. "At first, I sort of talked down to the kids, like they were kindergartners or something. Once I stopped doing that, the flute section really took off."

"Plus, I'm an awesome co-counselor," Sherman joked, elbowing Hope. "Admit it!"

"Never!" Hope smiled.

Mr. Byrd smiled, too. "Of course you're an awesome counselor, Sherman. That's why I chose you for this job."

I felt sort of funny then. Sherman knew his stuff when it came to playing the flute, and he was pretty great with the kids. It was easy to see why Mr. Byrd picked him as a counselor. But why'd he pick me?

As soon as the meeting was over, I decided to find out. "Mr. Byrd, can I talk to you for a sec?" I said when everyone was out of earshot.

"Absolutely, Morgan," he said. "What can I do for you?"

"It's just, when you first told us about camp, I was super excited," I began. "I mean, I thought

I'd be like Sherman. All of the kids love him. And the flute section kills it in ensemble practice every day. The clarinets, not so much. And tomorrow is Family Night. What am I doing wrong?"

Mr. Byrd thought for a minute. Then he said, "Instead of focusing on what you're doing wrong, tell me what you're doing right, Morgan."

I sort of laughed. "Most of the time, I don't feel like I'm doing anything right!"

Mr. Byrd smiled. "I can assure you that you are. For example, you and Baylor make a top-notch team. Right?"

"Right," I agreed. "Baylor and I get along great, and it's been fun getting to know her even better this week."

"See?" Mr. Byrd nodded.

"Yeah, but I'm not talking about Baylor and me. I'm talking about just me." I took a big breath then and told Mr. Byrd everything. All about how the clarinets hadn't shown any real progress this week, not like the flute or trumpet sections, at least. And how I wasn't this awesome music conductor like I'd hoped to be. Then the worst part was that I'd embarrassed Sam.

Mr. Byrd held up his hands. "Slow down, Morgan. First of all, I can understand that you feel as if you haven't made the progress you'd hoped to this week."

"You can?"

"Sure," he went on. "When I first became a teacher, I planned to have my band room filled with the world's greatest young musicians." He smiled. "Some of them were, and some of them weren't. But my point is, with such unreasonable expectations, I set myself up to fail. Does that make sense?"

I nodded. "Sometimes I'm such a perfectionist, I guess."

"There's nothing wrong with aiming for perfection when it comes to music," Mr. Byrd said. "Just give yourself permission to back off sometimes, too. Trust yourself. And as a counselor, trust your campers' abilities, too. Okay?"

"Okay," I agreed. "It's just, teaching isn't as easy as I thought it would be."

"Tell me about it!" Mr. Byrd laughed. "But it's oh, so worth it. And I know you're a hard worker, which is why you were an obvious choice when I selected camp counselors."

I smiled. Now I mostly felt better. "But what about Sam? He said he hates me."

"I'm sure Sam was upset," Mr. Byrd said. "Sometimes we say things we don't mean when we're upset. Give him some time to cool off."

I sighed. "All of the clarinet campers probably hate me."

"None of them hate you, Morgan. But they weren't too happy when you wanted them to practice through their lunch."

"They told you about that?" I asked.

Mr. Byrd nodded.

"Yeah, probably not one of my best ideas."

"If you really want to be a music conductor someday, here's some advice for you, Morgan."

Mr. Byrd had my full attention now. I leaned in, so I wouldn't miss a word.

"Even as a teacher, never stop learning," he said. Then he smiled. "And you've learned that you should never ask band students to skip lunch for more practice. They'll turn on you!"

I laughed then. A real laugh, maybe for the first time all week. And it felt good. "I won't forget that. Thanks, Mr. Byrd."

"You're welcome," he said. "Now, we have a band to lead here. And with Family Night tomorrow, we'd better get busy."

"Yes, sir," I said.

As soon as all of the campers were settled inside the classroom, it was time for small ensemble practice. Just like before, our clarinet section joined up with the flute and saxophone sections.

"I'll lead the campers through warm-ups," Sherman said. "Everyone, on your feet!"

See, when most people think of band warm-ups, they think of playing up and down scales, or even doing some breathing exercises. Not Sherman. Warm-ups to him meant physical exercise, like toe touches and jumping jacks. For real.

"Give me ten jumping jacks," Sherman called out. "Go!" He counted us through each one.

"Hey, I'm not as tired as I was on Monday," Matt said when we'd finished.

"Me neither," Julie Ann agreed.

Sherman smiled. "I told you! Exercise really does help your body prepare to play your instruments. And you all thought I was crazy."

"Nah, we still think you're crazy, Sherman," Zac joked, making circles around one ear with his finger.

The kids laughed when Sherman pretended to be offended. And they laughed even harder when Zac fell to the floor in front of Sherman and acted like he was begging for forgiveness.

"All is forgiven, good sir," Sherman said, doing this silly impersonation of a king. Even Baylor, me, and the other woodwind counselors laughed.

Then something sort of clicked in my brain. The kids responded so well to Sherman because he knew his stuff, but he wasn't pushy with it like I'd been all week. Sherman made things fun. The kids actually wanted to learn when it was fun.

And I mean, things couldn't be all fun all the time. Sherman seemed to know that, too. Sherman had something that I didn't. Balance. Why hadn't I noticed that before?

After Sherman had us run in place and jump an imaginary rope, Hope took over. "Assemble your instruments, and we'll begin with a concert B-flat scale."

While the kids warmed up their instruments, Zac said, "I saw you talking to Mr. Byrd."

I nodded.

"So did he say anything about which section is better, the saxophones or the clarinets?"

I smiled. Zac still hadn't forgotten about saying that his section would be better than mine and Baylor's. I played it cool, though. "I saw him talking to you earlier this week, too. Why don't you fill me in on that?" Baylor would probably be proud of my detective-ing since I was trying to make Zac give up some information before I did.

"Wanna know the truth?" Zac asked.

I nodded.

"Mr. Byrd wanted to tell me he was thrilled with how well the saxes played 'Pink Popsicles.'"

"Yeah, I bet he was thrilled," I said. "And probably surprised, too, huh?"

At first, I didn't think Zac would come clean about that, but he totally did. "I told Mr. Byrd it was all a fluke," he admitted. "It was lucky for me, the kids in my group already knew that song."

"Mr. DiMeo taught them, right?"

Zac's eyes widened. "You knew?"

"Not at first," I said. "But later, Lincoln told Baylor and me all about it."

He rolled his eyes. "Leave it to Baylor, the star reporter, to figure it out."

I smiled.

Zac said, "I guess neither of our sections have exactly blown the other one out of the water, huh?"

"Nope, not exactly," I agreed.

Neither of us said anything for a minute after that. Then Zac finally asked, "So what did Mr. Byrd talk to you about?"

"He gave me some advice. I should never ask band students to practice on an empty stomach," I said, laughing.

"Have you lost it?" Zac said. "That doesn't even make any sense."

It made total sense to me at the time.

"You know what, Zac?"

He shook his head.

"Instead of trying to blow each other's section out of the water, we should totally join forces and blow these two songs out of the water. Our sections will kill it tomorrow at Family Night."

Zac thought about it for a second. Then he nodded. "I'm digging it." He held out his hand, and we shook on it. "Partners."

"Partners," I repeated. "So now will you give me back my clipboard?"

"I'm not kidding. I seriously don't have it," Zac said.

Then who did? I guessed Sam. But I couldn't think about it anymore right now because Hope asked me to lead the ensemble in playing "The Llama's Grand Mama."

Only this time, I didn't lead the group on my own. Zac and I worked together.

It turned out to be the best practice we'd had all week. Seriously!

Chapter 10

MUSICAL MAGIC

"Can you believe it's Friday, Morgan?" Baylor asked the next day.

Really, I couldn't. The week at camp had flown by. Now in a few short weeks, school would start back. And then I'd get to do what I love to do every day: play my clarinet with the rest of the band!

But first things first. This was our last day of camp, and it ended with Family Night. We still had a ton of things to do before tonight.

Mr. Byrd started things off with, "To celebrate an amazing week at camp, we'll begin our day with an extra fun activity. I call it the Olympic Games, band style!"

"Are we cycling with our instruments, or something?" Connor asked.

"No way, it's all about synchronized swimming with them," I said, performing a pretend water routine. Baylor and Zac joined in, and we twirled around our imaginary pool with our fake instruments.

Tatum and Sam cracked up when we all pretended to splash into each other. It felt good to end the week with Sam smiling again.

"Maybe we'll save that event for next year's camp," Mr. Byrd said, smiling too. Then he explained how to play the different games and put us counselors in charge of leading them.

For my game, the campers would throw a javelin through a ring of fire. Not really. But they would toss a drumstick through some plastic rings with red, orange, and yellow construction paper taped all around to look like flames.

"Line up behind Sam," I said, handing him a drumstick since he was the first one in my line. "Everyone gets three tries."

On the first try, Sam almost got it. On the second try, he didn't even get close.

"This is harder than it looks," Sam said.

I gave him a thumbs-up. "You've got this."

Sam closed one eye, took aim, and let the drumstick fly. It sailed right past me, hit a ring, and bounced to the side. Before the drumstick hit the floor, I gave it a little help to get it through the ring.

"And Sam scores!" I whooped, pumping my fists in the air.

"Hey, you're different today!" Aliyah said.

I pretended to check out my clothes. "Different?" I said, acting confused.

Mischa grinned. "Not your clothes, silly!"

"Yeah," Sam added. "You're acting different today. Like, more fun."

I scrunched my nose. "You really think so?"

Mischa and Aliyah both nodded. So did Sam.

"I wish I'd been more fun all week," I said. "I'm sorry for being so focused that I wasn't."

"That's okay," Connor said. And Tatum sort of smiled.

Next they lined up to play the game beside mine. Zac was in charge of the Reed Race where two campers competed to slide reeds down the table to see whose crossed the finish line first.

After the campers played all of the games, we separated into different sections. Our clarinet group went to our usual spot near the window.

Before I started talking, Mischa said, "Look behind you, Morgan."

"It's not another spider, is it?" I asked, slowly turning around.

It wasn't. Lying on the window sill was a package. "What's this?" I asked.

"Open it," Tatum said, smiling.

I pulled off the bow and stuck it on my head. Then I ripped apart the paper, tore open the box, and dug past some tissue paper. "My clipboard! You guys found it."

"Not exactly," Sam began.

And I knew where this was going. He was so mad at me that he took off with my clipboard, and now he was sorry.

"It's okay, Sam," I said. He didn't have to explain. Really. "We all do dumb stuff sometimes."

"I'm the one who did something dumb," Tatum spoke up.

"Seriously?" I looked at Tatum and then back at my clipboard. "But why did you take it?"

She bit her lip before answering. "Sam is one of my best friends. When he got upset at you, I took your clipboard to sort of get even. But when Sam found out, he made me give it back. And my mom grounded me for a week." She looked down at her flip-flops. "I'm sorry, Morgan. I really didn't mean anything by it."

"It's no problem, Tatum," I said. "Seriously."

She looked up then. "I decorated the back of it for you. I hope you don't mind."

I hadn't noticed, but when I flipped it over, I saw that Tatum had sticker-ized it. My name was spelled out in pink letters, surrounded by music note stickers.

"If you don't like it, you can just peel them off," Tatum said.

"No, I love it! Every time I use my clipboard, I'll think of you." I smiled. "All of you."

Baylor leaned over and made a check in the air. "There's one mystery solved."

"Yeah." I nodded. But we still hadn't figured out the biggest mystery of all. How did Zac and Sam know each other? Maybe we would never crack that case.

After that, the rest of the day passed in a giant blur of ensemble practice and group practice and hugs as everyone told each other good-bye one last time before Family Night.

That evening, the campers and their families gathered at the community center. Everyone walked around, checking out the artwork on display that some campers had made.

Baylor, Hope, Zac, and I were looking at this super cool dolphin painting when a lady came up and said, "Zac! Thanks for hanging out with Sam. He's talked about you all week. And someone named Morgan."

I raised my hand. "That's me."

"Hi, I'm Sam's mom." She smiled. "He says you're way cool."

"Really?" I was surprised. Maybe Mr. Byrd was right, and Sam didn't really mean it when he said he hated me. "I think Sam is way cool, too." I held out my hand for a fist bump. "Friends?"

Sam smiled. "Friends!"

And when they went on, Baylor said, "Spill it, Zac! This proves that you already knew Sam. But what we can't figure out is how."

"Seriously? Miss Super Star Detective can't figure something out," Zac said, smiling.

"C'mon," I said. "What gives? We want to solve this mystery."

At first, Zac seemed hesitant. But then he said, "Sam and I know each other because sometimes I help out at this after-school program for younger kids who have dyslexia, okay?" He paused. "I like to hang out with them because I'm dyslexic, too."

Now Baylor and I were quiet until she said, "That's right. You told me once that sometimes the music notes get all mixed up when you play."

Zac nodded.

I was totally surprised. "Is that what you meant when you said we all have stuff to deal with?"

"You got it," Zac said.

"But why keep it a secret that you and Sam know each other?" I asked. "Like, on that first day of camp when you acted like you didn't know his name until you read his name tag."

Zac shrugged. "That was totally Sam's idea. Maybe he was afraid if the other kids figured out how we knew each other, they'd find out about his dyslexia, too. And hey, I get it. It's not something you want to talk about all the time. You know?"

Yeah, I really did know.

"So you're like a mentor at this after-school program," Baylor went on. "That means you're not a goof-off all the time, Zac."

"Whatever!" He grinned. "Just do me a favor and don't go blabbing it all over school."

"I promise," Baylor said.

I nodded. "Me too."

"Good! Because if you tell, I'll call my lawyer," Zac joked.

We all laughed, until Mr. Byrd motioned us into the auditorium.

"Tonight, we celebrate the fine arts," Mrs. Harman said into the microphone at center stage. "We also celebrate these fine young ladies and gentleman who have worked so hard this week to share their talents with us."

That set off a round of applause across the auditorium.

Mrs. Harman continued with, "Tonight's entertainment begins with a skit performed by our theater troupe. Enjoy!"

The curtains rose on a dramatic scene. The set was dark as a voice spoke about being bullied. Then other voices rang out words of hope as the lights came on, dimly at first. Then brighter as the bullying chains were broken.

As the skit ended, everyone rose to their feet, clapping and cheering.

"Wonderful job, campers," Mrs. Harman said, back at center stage once more. "Next, to delight your ears, please welcome our musical troupe."

The counselors had been hanging out with the band campers offstage. Now, we encouraged them as they made their way onstage.

"Go for it, dudes!" Sherman said.

"You'll sound amazing!" Baylor chimed in.

And I said, "No matter what, have fun!"

Zac looked surprised. "Seriously?"

"Yeah," I nodded. "I've sort of killed the camp fun this week."

He joked, "No way!"

"Whatever." I smiled. "But seriously, once I figured out how to balance fun with skills, the clarinet section rocked. They've really got their music down."

"You mean the saxophone section rocked. Right?" Zac teased.

I crossed my arms. "I suppose they did, too."

"Hey!" Sherman looked offended. "What about the flutes?"

I laughed. "And the flutes."

"Don't forget the trumpets, *mademoiselle*," Lem added.

"Yep, they rocked, too." I said. "So did the trombones, the French horns, and the percussion section."

"Here's a scoop for you. It takes all of the instruments working together to make a great band," Baylor said, pointing toward the stage. "Just listen."

The campers really did sound amazing. So they weren't perfect, like I'd hoped they'd be when camp first began. But looking out at the smiles on their families' faces, I knew being perfect didn't matter. At least, not as much as it did before.

"I never thought it would happen, but everything finally came together," Zac said. "Like magic."

"You mean, like musical magic," I said.

And we both smiled.